a Little Golden Book® Collection

Animal Tales

A GOLDEN BOOK • NEW YORK

🌸 A GOLDEN BOOK • NEW YORK

Compilation copyright © 2004 by Random House, Inc.
The Saggy Baggy Elephant copyright © 1947, renewed 1975 by Random House, Inc.
The Kitten Who Thought He Was a Mouse copyright © 1951, 1954, renewed 1979, 1982 by Random House, Inc.
How the Leopard Got Its Spots copyright © 2000 by Random House, Inc.
Mister Dog copyright © 1952, renewed 1980 by Random House, Inc.
Animal Orchestra copyright © 1958, renewed 1986 by Random House, Inc.
The Lion's Paw copyright © 1960, renewed 1988 by Random House, Inc.
Baby Animals copyright © 1952, 1956, renewed 1980, 1984 by Random House, Inc.
The Golden Egg Book copyright © 1947, renewed 1975 by Random House, Inc.
Animal Friends copyright © 1953, renewed 1981 by Random House, Inc.
The Big Brown Bear copyright © 1947, renewed 1975 by Random House, Inc.
Home for a Bunny copyright © 1956, 1961, renewed 1984, 1989 by Random House, Inc.
How the Camel Got Its Hump copyright © 2001 by Random House, Inc.
Tawny Scrawny Lion copyright © 1952, renewed 1980 by Random House, Inc.
All rights reserved under International and Pan-American Copyright Conventions. Published in the United States by
Golden Books, an imprint of Random House Children's Books, a division of Random House, Inc., New York, and simultaneously
in Canada by Random House of Canada Limited, Toronto. Golden Books, A Golden Book, a Little Golden Book, and
the G colophon are registered trademarks of Random House, Inc.
The Saggy Baggy Elephant is a registered trademark of Random House, Inc.
Tawny Scrawny Lion is a trademark of Random House, Inc.
Library of Congress Control Number: 2004101307
ISBN: 0-375-83128-2
www.goldenbooks.com
Printed in the United States of America   First Random House Edition 2004
Book design by Roberta Ludlow
10 9 8 7 6 5 4 3 2

Contents

THE SAGGY BAGGY
ELEPHANT

A happy little elephant was dancing through the jungle. He thought he was dancing beautifully, one-two-three-kick. But whenever he went one-two-three, his big feet pounded so that they shook the whole jungle. And whenever he went kick, he kicked over a tree or a bush.

The little elephant danced along leaving wreckage behind him, until one day, he met a parrot.

"Why are you shaking the jungle all to pieces?" cried the parrot, who had never before seen an elephant. "What kind of animal are you, anyway?"

The little elephant said, "I don't know what kind of animal I am. I live all alone in the jungle. I dance and I kick—and I call myself Sooki. It's a good-sounding name, and it fits me, don't you think?"

"Maybe," answered the parrot, "but if it does it's the only thing that *does* fit you. Your ears are too big for you, and your nose is way too big for you. And your skin is *much,* MUCH too big for you. It's baggy and saggy. You should call yourself Saggy-Baggy!"

Sooki sighed. His pants *did* look pretty wrinkled.

"I'd be glad to improve myself," he said, "but I don't know how to go about it. What shall I do?"

"I can't tell you. I never saw anything like you in all my life!" replied the parrot.

The little elephant tried to smooth out his skin.
He rubbed it with his trunk. That did no good.

He pulled up his pants legs—but they fell right back into dozens of wrinkles.

It was very disappointing, and the parrot's saucy laugh didn't help a bit.

Just then a tiger came walking along. He was a beautiful, sleek tiger. His skin fit him like a glove.

Sooki rushed up to him and said:

"Tiger, please tell me why your skin fits so well! The parrot says mine is all baggy and saggy,  and I do want to make it fit me like yours fits you!"

The tiger didn't care a fig about Sooki's troubles, but he did feel flattered and important, and he did feel just a little mite hungry.

"My skin always did fit," said the tiger. "Maybe it's because I take a lot of exercise. But . . ." added the tiger, ". . . if you don't care for exercise, I shall be delighted to nibble a few of those extra pounds of skin off for you!"

"Oh no, thank you! No, thank you!" cried Sooki. "I love exercise! Just watch me!"

Sooki ran until he was well beyond reach.

Then he did somersaults and rolled on his back. He walked on his hind legs and he walked on his front legs.

When Sooki wandered down to the river to get a big drink of water, he met the parrot. The parrot laughed harder than ever.

"I tried exercising," sighed the little elephant. "Now I don't know what to do."

"Soak in the water the way the crocodile does," laughed the parrot. "Maybe your skin will shrink."

So Sooki tramped straight into the water.

14

But before he had soaked nearly long enough to shrink his skin, a great big crocodile came swimming up, snapping his fierce jaws and looking greedily at Sooki's tender ears.

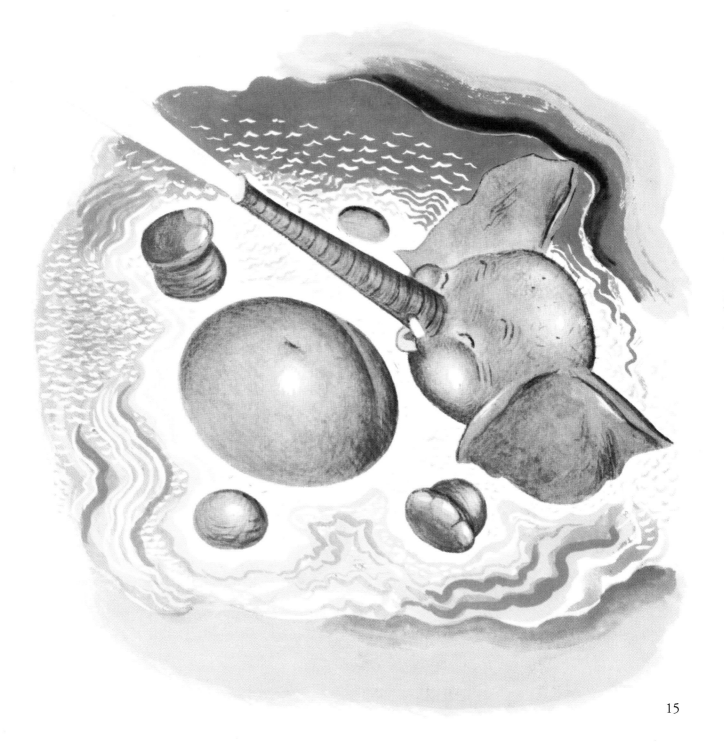

The little elephant clambered up the bank and ran away, feeling very discouraged.

"I'd better hide in a dark place where my bags and sags and creases and wrinkles won't show," he said.

By and by he found a deep dark cave, and with a heavy sigh he tramped inside and sat down.

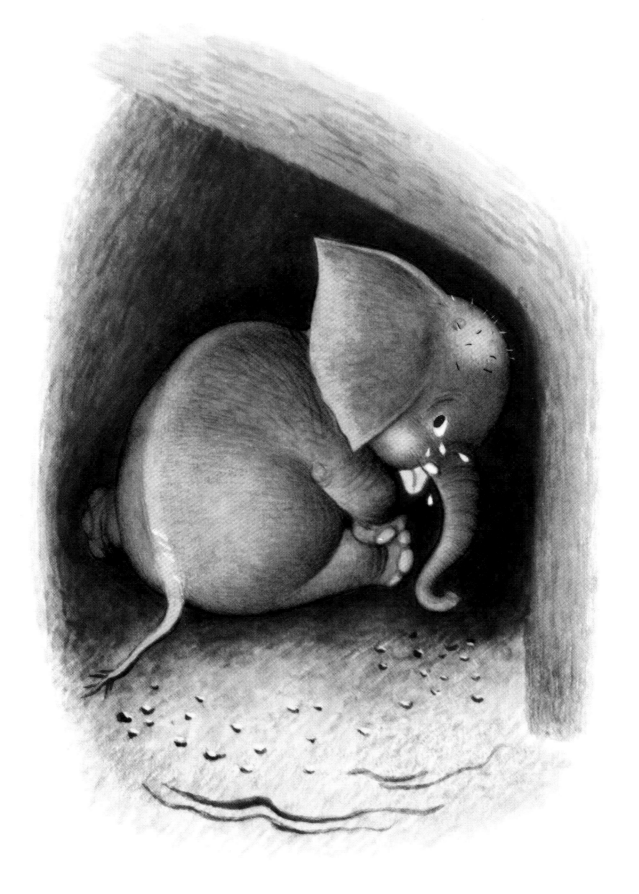

Suddenly, he heard a fierce growling and grumbling and snarling. He peeped out of the cave and saw a lion padding down the path.

"I'm hungry!" roared the lion. "I haven't had a thing to eat today. Not a thing except a thin, bony antelope, and a puny monkey—and a buffalo, but such a tough one! And two turtles, but you can't count turtles. There's nothing much to eat between those saucers they wear for clothes! I'm *hungry!* I could eat an *elephant!*"

And he began to pad straight toward the dark cave where the little elephant was hidden.

"This is the end of me, sags, bags, wrinkles and all," thought Sooki, and he let out one last, trumpeting bellow!

Just as he did, the jungle was filled with a terrible crashing and an awful stomping. A whole herd of great gray wrinkled elephants came charging up, and the big hungry lion jumped up in the air, turned around, and ran away as fast as he could go.

Sooki peeped out of the cave and all the big elephants smiled at him. Sooki thought they were the most beautiful creatures he had ever seen.

"I wish I looked just like you," he said.

"You do," grinned the big elephants. "You're a perfectly dandy little elephant!"

And that made Sooki so happy that he began to

dance one-two-three-kick through the jungle, with all those big, brave, friendly elephants behind him. The saucy parrot watched them dance. But this time he didn't laugh, not even to himself.

THE KITTEN
who thought he was a
MOUSE

There were five Miggses: Mother and
Father Miggs and Lester and two sisters.

They had, as field mice usually do, an outdoor
nest for summer in an empty lot, and an indoor
nest for winter in a nearby house.

They were very surprised, one summer day, to find a strange bundle in their nest—a small gray and black bundle of fur and ears and legs, with eyes not yet open. They knew by its mewing that the bundle must be a kitten, a lost kitten with no family and no name.

"Poor kitty," said the sisters.
"Let him stay with us," said Lester.
"But a *cat!*" said Mother Miggs.

"Why not?" said Father Miggs.

"We can bring him up to be a good mouse. He need never find out that he is really a cat. You'll see—he'll be a good thing for this family."

"Let's call him Mickey," said Lester.

And that's how Mickey Miggs found his new family and a name.

After his eyes opened, Mickey began to grow up just as mice do, eating all kinds of seeds and bugs, drinking from puddles, and sleeping in a cozy pile of brother and sister mice.

Father Miggs showed him his first tomcat—at a safe distance—and warned him to "keep away from all cats and dogs and people."

Mickey saw his first mousetrap—"The most dangerous thing of all," said Mother Miggs— when they moved to the indoor nest that fall.

He was too clumsy to steal bait from
traps himself, so Lester and the sisters had
to share with him what they stole.

But Mickey was useful in fooling the household cat, Hazel. He practiced up on meowing—for usually, of course, he squeaked—and became clever at what he thought was *imitating* a cat.

He would hide in a dark corner and then, *"Meow! Meow!"* he'd cry. Hazel would poke around, leaving the pantry shelves unguarded while she looked for the other cat. That gave Lester and his sisters a chance to make a raid on the leftovers.

Poor Hazel! She knew she heard, even smelled, another cat, and sometimes she saw cat's eyes shining in a corner. But no cat ever came out to meet her.

How could she know that Mickey didn't know he was a cat at all, and that he feared Hazel as much as the mousiest mouse would!

And so Mickey Miggs grew, becoming a better mouse all the time and enjoying his life. He loved cheese, bacon, and cake crumbs.

He got especially good at smelling out potato skins, and
led the sisters and Lester straight to them every time.

"A wholesome and uncatlike food," said Mother Miggs
to Father Miggs approvingly. "Mickey is doing well."

And Father Miggs said to Mother Miggs, "I told you so!"

Then one day, coming from a nap in the wastepaper basket, Mickey met the children of the house, Peggy and Paul.

"Ee-eeeeek!" Mickey squeaked in terror. He dashed along the walls of the room, looking for his mousehole.

"It's a kitten!" cried Peggy, as Mickey squeezed through the hole.

"But it acts like a mouse," said Paul.

The children could not understand why the kitten had been so mouselike, but they decided to try to make friends with him.

That night, as Mickey came out of his hole, he nearly tripped over something lying right there in front of him. He sniffed at it. It was a dish, and in the dish was something to drink.

"What is it?" asked Mickey. Lester didn't know, but timidly tried a little. "No good," he said, shaking his whiskers.

Mickey tried it, tried some more, then some more and some more and more and more—until it was all gone.

"Mmmmmmmmmm!" he said. "What wonderful stuff."

"It's probably poison and you'll get sick," said Lester disgustedly. But it wasn't poison and Mickey had a lovely feeling in his stomach from drinking it. It was milk, of course. And every night that week Mickey found a saucer of milk outside that same hole. He lapped up every drop.

"He drank it, he drank it!" cried Peggy and Paul happily each morning. They began to set out a saucerful in the daytime, too.

At first Mickey would drink the milk only when he was sure Peggy and Paul were nowhere around. Soon he grew bolder and began to trust them in the room with him.

And soon he began to let them come nearer and nearer and nearer still.

Then one day he found himself scooped up and held in Peggy's arms. He didn't feel scared. He felt fine. And he felt a queer noise rumble up his back and all through him. It was Mickey's first purr.

Peggy and Paul took Mickey to a shiny glass on the wall and held him close in front of it. Mickey, who had never seen a mirror, saw a cat staring at him there, a cat in Paul's hands, where he thought *he* was. He began to cry, and his cry, instead of being a squeak, was a mewing wail.

Finally Mickey began to understand that he
was not a mouse like Lester and his sisters, but a
cat like Hazel.

He stayed with Peggy and Paul that night,
trying not to be afraid of his own cat-self. He
still didn't quite believe it all, however, and next
morning he crept back through his old hole
straight to Mother Miggs.

"Am I really a cat?" he cried.

"Yes," said Mother Miggs sadly. And she told him the whole story of how he was adopted and brought up as a mouse. "We loved you and wanted you to love us," she explained. "It was the only safe and fair way to bring you up."

After talking with Mother Miggs, Mickey decided to be a cat in all ways. He now lives with Peggy and Paul, who also love him, and who can give him lots of good milk, and who aren't afraid of his purr or his meow.

Mickey can't really forget his upbringing, however. He takes an old rubber mouse of Peggy's to bed with him.

He often visits the Miggses in the indoor nest,
where he nibbles cheese tidbits and squeaks about
old times.

And of course he sees to it that Hazel no longer
prowls in the pantry at night.

"Oh, I'm so fat and stuffed from eating so much in Hazel's pantry," Father Miggs often says happily to Mother Miggs. "I always said our Mickey would be a good thing for the family—and he is!"

reetings! I am Professor Polka—expert in the history of dots and spots and related topics. For years and years, people have been trying to figure out how the leopard got its spots. They've come up with some wild stories. Here are a few:

One tale from East Africa says that two lion cubs,
let's call them Burt and Giggles, once watched some
humans decorating their faces and bodies with paint.
"That looks like fun!" Giggles said.
Burt agreed.

As soon as the humans left, the cubs started painting each other. Giggles used his paws to put black spots all over Burt. Then it was Burt's turn to paint Giggles.

But before Burt could finish putting spots on his
brother, they heard the humans coming back. Burt was
so scared, he accidentally spilled the pot of paint over
Giggles's head!

The cubs quickly ran home to their cozy lion cave.
But the mother lion would not let them in.
  "You are not lions!" she roared.
  And, in fact, Mom was right! The half-black Giggles
had become the first hyena. And Burt, with his
gorgeous spots, had become the very first leopard.

Here is another story. This one is by the great British writer, Rudyard Kipling. According to Kipling, the Sandy Leopard was so good at hunting in the Sandy Savanna that he scared off the Sandy Wildebeest, the Sandy Zebra, and the Sandy Giraffe.

That is when the Sandy Leopard became the Hungry Sandy Leopard!

His former meals had fled to the Dark, Stripy, Splotchy Forest where they hid under the trees and bushes. After a while, the sun, which peeked through the leaves and twigs and around the shadows, darkened the animals' skin in certain places.

The Sandy Wildebeest, the Sandy Zebra, and the Sandy Giraffe became the Dark Wildebeest, the Stripy Zebra, and the Splotchy Giraffe.

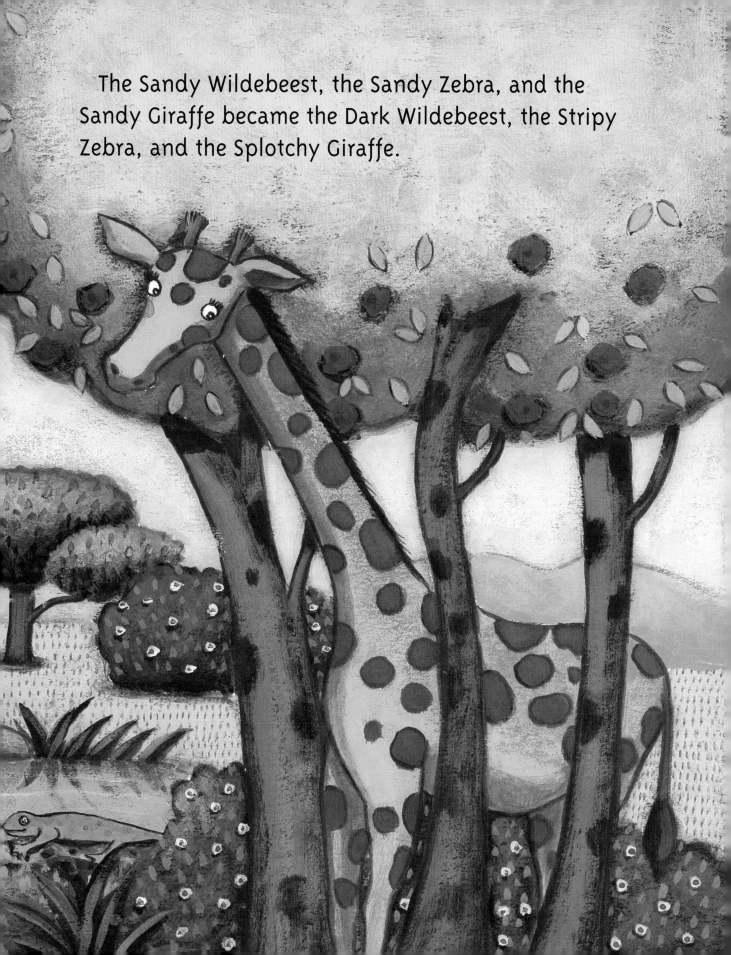

When the Hungry Sandy Leopard came into the
forest for dinner, he couldn't see any of the animals.
Their stripes and splotches helped them blend right
into their surroundings.

The Sandy Leopard discovered their trick and soon realized he needed to blend in, too, or else he could easily become someone else's dinner!

And that is how Kipling thinks the leopard got its spots.

Another legend tells us that back when the world was new, Leopard had no spots.

Leopard loved to stretch out on a shady tree limb, wait for a tasty critter to come by, and then . . .

Pounce!

Leopard was so good at pouncing that fewer and fewer animals dared to eat leaves from his tree. And the tree was so grateful to Leopard that it became his friend. If Leopard was hot, the tree would fan him with its branches.

Soon all the animals wised up. They learned to stay away from Leopard's tree, so Leopard had to come down from the tree to hunt. By now Leopard was very hungry!

But when Leopard came out of cover, he was easy to see in the forest. All the animals ran away from him and hid.

"Hunting is such hard work!" complained Leopard to the tree. "If only I could wear your shadows. Then I could surprise the animals and . . . pounce!"

"What a marvelous idea!" exclaimed the tree. "Here, take these leaf shadows. I have plenty."

Leopard licked the leaf shadows and stuck them on his fur. Soon he was covered in spots and could not be seen easily by the other animals! Now Leopard could pounce anywhere in the forest.

And whenever he is not pouncing, Leopard
returns to his beloved tree, which is where you'll
find him to this day.

MISTER DOG

Once upon a time there was a funny dog
named Crispin's Crispian. He was named
Crispin's Crispian because—

he belonged to himself.

In the mornings, he woke himself up and he went
to the icebox and gave himself some bread and milk.
He was a funny old dog. He liked strawberries.

Then he took himself for a walk. And he went wherever he wanted to go.

But one morning he didn't know where he wanted to go.

"Just walk and sooner or later you'll get somewhere," he said to himself.

Soon he came to a country where there were
lots of dogs. They barked at him and he
barked back. Then they all played together.

But he still wanted to go somewhere, so he walked on until he came to a country where there were lots of cats and rabbits.

The cats and rabbits jumped in the air and ran. So Crispian jumped in the air and ran after them.

He didn't catch them because he ran bang into a little boy.

"Who are you and who do you belong to?" asked the little boy.

"I am Crispin's Crispian and I belong to myself," said Crispian. "Who and what are you?"

"I am a boy," said the boy, "and I belong to myself."

"I am so glad," said Crispin's Crispian. "Come and live with me."

Then they went to a butcher shop—"to get
his poor dog a bone," Crispian said.

Now, since Crispin's Crispian belonged to himself,
he gave himself the bone and trotted home with it.
And the boy's little boy bought a big lamb chop
and a bright green vegetable and trotted home with
Crispin's Crispian.

Crispin's Crispian lived in a two-story doghouse in a garden. And in his two-story doghouse, he had a little fur living room with a warm fire that crackled all winter and went out in the summer.

His house was always warm. His house had a chimney for the smoke to go out. And upstairs there was a little bedroom with a bed in it and a place for his leash and a pillow under which he hid his bones.

And there was plenty of room in his house for the boy to live there with him.

Crispian had a little kitchen upstairs in his two-story doghouse where he fixed himself a good dinner three times a day because he liked to eat. He liked steaks and chops and roast beef and chopped meat and raw eggs.

This evening he made a bone soup with lots of meat in it. He gave some to the boy, and the boy liked it. The boy didn't give Crispian his chop bone, but he put some of his bright green vegetable in the soup.

And what did Crispian do with his dinner?
Did he put it in his stomach?
Yes, indeed.
He chewed it up and swallowed it into his
little fat stomach.

And what did the little boy do with his dinner?
Did he put it in his stomach?
Yes, indeed.
He chewed it up and swallowed it into his
little fat stomach.

     Crispin's Crispian was a *conservative.*
He liked everything at the right time—
   dinner at dinner time,
   lunch at lunchtime,
   breakfast in time for breakfast,
   and sunrise at sunrise,
   and sunset at sunset.
   And at bedtime—
At bedtime, he liked everything in its
own place—
   the cup in the saucer,
   the chair under the table,
   the stars in the heavens,
   the moon in the sky,
   and himself in his own little bed.

And then what did he do?

Then he curled in a warm little heap and went to sleep. And he dreamed his own dreams.

That was what the dog who belonged to himself did.

And what did the boy who belonged to himself do?
The boy who belonged to himself curled in a
warm little heap and went to sleep. And he dreamed
his own dreams.

That was what the boy who belonged to himself did.

GOOD NIGHT
AND
SWEET DREAMS.

Animal Orchestra

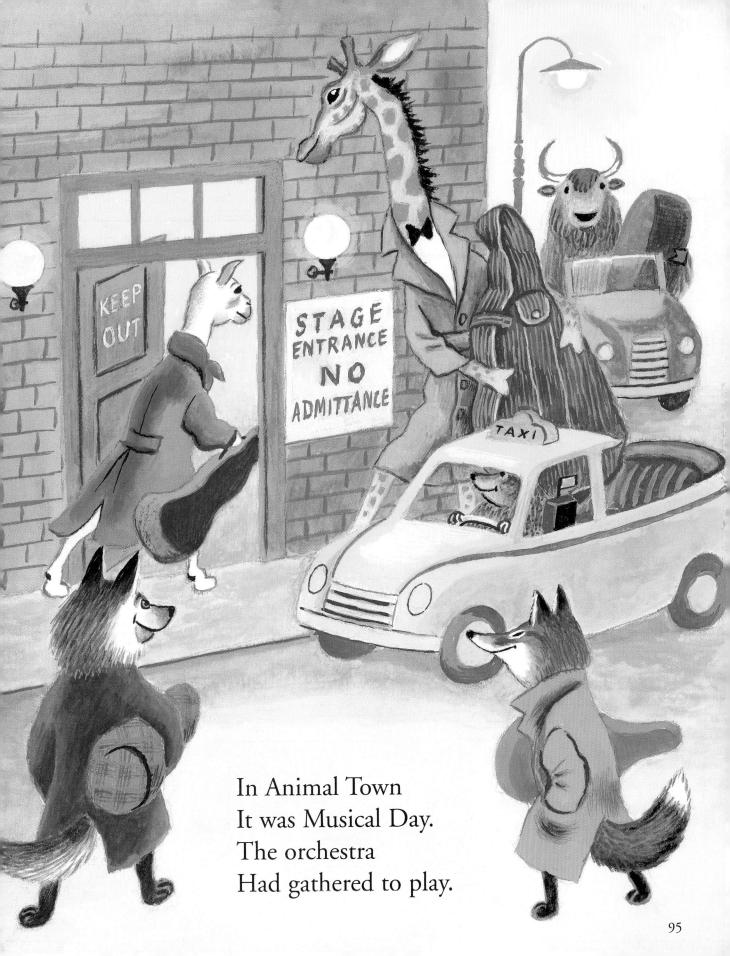

In Animal Town
It was Musical Day.
The orchestra
Had gathered to play.

Everyone came
To hear and to see.

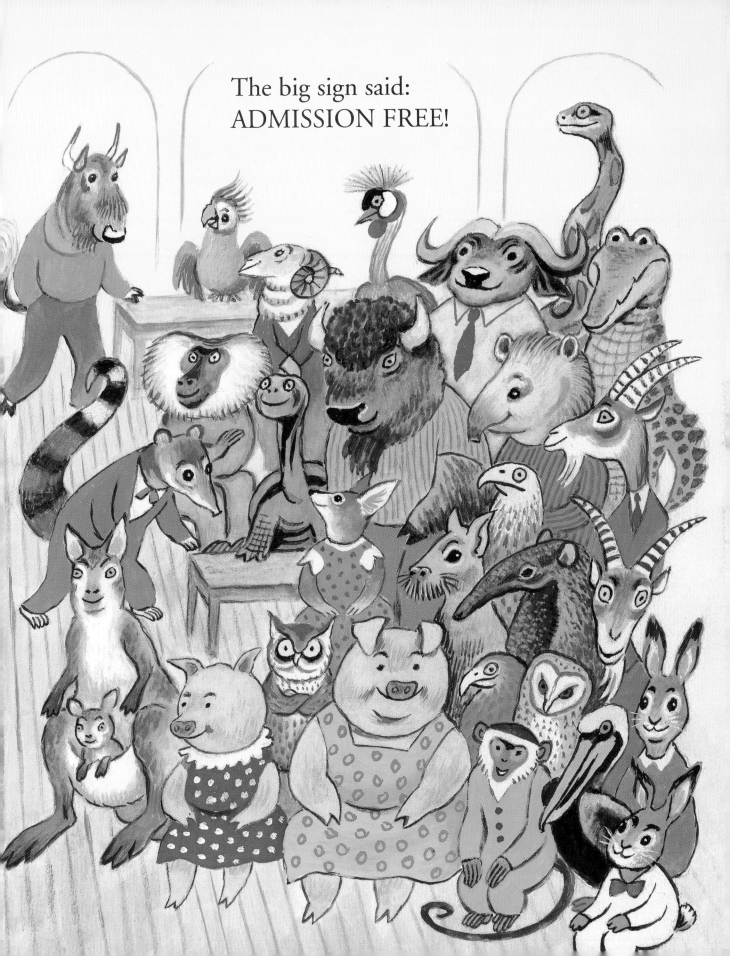

The big sign said:
ADMISSION FREE!

Up to the platform
Each animal went,

98

And proudly carried
His instrument.

Then came the conductor
With stick in his hand—
The handsomest Hippo
In Animal Land.
He tapped his foot.
He waved his hand,
And cried to the players:
"Strike up the band!"

The gray Seals barked.
They lifted their fins,
And tweedled upon
Their violins.

The spotted Giraffes—
The oddest fellows—
Zoomed and zoomed
On their yellow cellos.

The Lion bugled;
The Rhino fluted;

The Leopard harped;
The Tiger tooted.

The Monkey wiggled
A brass trombone.
The Llama blew
A saxophone.

The Elephant
Kept trumpeting.
The Camel plucked
His mandolin string.

Upon his cymbals
The Bear clang-clanged.

Upon his guitar
The Fox twang-twanged!

The Yak beat the drum;
The Wolf played the fife.
Each beast was enjoying
The time of his life.

They whistled! They fiddled!
They thumped! They blew!

What a roar! What a din!
What a great to-do!

The animal girls—
The animal boys—
The animal audience
Made a great noise.

They slapped their tails,
They clapped their paws,
And that is how
They made applause!

The conductor bowed,
And bowed and bowed.

All of the orchestra
Players were proud.

The Hippo was happy
On Musical Day,
For everyone shouted:
"Hip-HIPPO-ray!"

The Lion's Paw

Ow! roared the lion.
"There is a thorn in my paw.
Who will take it out?"

"Not I," said the solid rhinoceros.
"I am sharpening my pointed horn."

"Not I," said the startled kudu.
"I am racing away from here!"

"Not I," whispered the tall
giraffe among the tip-top leaves.

"Not I," said the bouncing baboon.
"I am having too much fun."

"Who will take the thorn out?"
asked the crowned crane.

"Not I," said the hippopotamus.
"I am cooling off in the mud."

"Not I," said the striped zebra.
"I am kicking up my heels."

"Not I," said the bright-eyed monkey.
"I am swinging by my tail."

"Not I," said the big gorilla.
"I am scratching away my fleas."

"Not I," said the elegant gazelle.
"I am leaping across the veld."

"Will no one remove the thorn?"
called the ibis by the purple pool.

"Not I," said the slippery crocodile,
smiling a hungry smile.

"Not I," said the trumpeting elephant.
"I am taking a shower."

"Not I," said the spotted leopard.
"I am slinking through the shade."

"Not I," said the solemn buffalo.
"I have too much work to do."

"Who will help the lion?" cried the ostrich running over the desert sands.

"Not I," said the sulky camel.
"I am chewing my chewy cud."

"Not I," said the swooping vulture.
"I'm busy hunting a meal."

"Not I," said the fast cheetah.
"I'm busy hunting, too."

"I will," said the little mouse.
And she did!

Baby Animals

Baby Bear holds his toes. He wants to be a
circus bear when he grows up. He wants to
make all the children laugh.

Baby Squirrel has come to see what
his little cousin the chipmunk is so busy
doing at the end of the long branch.

Baby Chipmunk has a delicious nut and he is going to stuff it into his cheek before the baby squirrel gets it. They both like nuts to eat.

Baby Fox is full of mischief. He is hoping he will find a sleepy rabbit to chase, but the rabbits are hiding.

Baby Lamb is dancing over the hills
and meadows. It is spring and everyone
wants to dance after the cold winter.

Baby Opossum is pretending to be dead. If a big bad dog comes along he will play dead and the dog will go away.

Baby Skunk is fooled by his playmate
lying so still.

Baby Lion roars "Ahrrroum" just like his father. One day he hopes he will be king of the jungle.

Baby Tiger says, "You frighten me."
Baby Tiger looks like a great big kitten,
and he loves to play like one.

Baby Giraffe is so tall that he has to bend down to stay in the picture. He never makes a sound, and he can run very fast.

Baby Monkey swings from branch to branch. He holds on with his two hands, with his two feet, and with his tail.

Baby Orang-utan also lives in the trees. He is putting a leaf on his head to keep the sun off.

Baby Kangaroo hops like six rabbits.
He uses his big tail to keep his balance,
so he won't fall.

Baby Koala Bear lives in Australia like Baby Kangaroo. He sleeps in the eucalyptus tree at night and eats its leaves in the daytime.

Baby Woodchuck has been asleep all
winter long. Now he is eating tender
grass and a small, tasty root. Soon he
will be very plump.

Baby Mink has just caught his first fish.
He is going to show it to his mother and
then eat it for breakfast.

Baby Rabbit has hopped away from his mother's side. His eyes are wide open. He sees a big bumblebee. "I don't think I will go any farther," he says.

Baby Racoon washes his apple. He never eats anything until he has washed it first. He even washes a fish.

Baby Camel walks very well and can go for a day without drinking. He keeps food and water in his fat humps.

Baby Owl says, "Whoooooooo's undressed
and whoooooooo's in bed? Whoooooooo's
awake and whooooooo's asleep?"

The Golden Egg Book

Once there was a little bunny.
He was all alone.
One day he found an egg.
He could hear something moving
    inside the egg.
What was it?

Maybe a little boy,

Maybe another bunny,

Maybe an elephant,

Maybe a mouse.

Who could tell what he would find?
And how would a little bunny know?
But there was something
    inside that egg.

He could hear
something moving.

He shook it.

Then the bunny
pushed the egg
with his foot.

He jumped on top
of the egg.

He climbed a tree and threw nuts at it.

He rolled the egg down a hill.
But still it didn't break.
And whatever was
in the egg
didn't come out.

So the bunny
    threw a rock
    at the egg.
But because he was only a
    little bunny, it was a very
    little rock and he didn't
    throw it very hard and
    the egg didn't break.

Pick

Pick

Pick

Something was trying to get out of that egg.
The bunny sat very still and watched
through his shining eyes.

He sat very still and listened
with his big soft ears—

Pick

Pick

Pick

Then the little bunny
began to yawn.
And he yawned
and he yawned.

The egg was
very quiet.

He curled up all sleepy and warm
    close to the egg and went to sleep.
He went to sleep because he was
    so sleepy.

                    Then . . .

Pick

    Pick

        Pick

and

    Peck

        Peck

        Peck

And crackety CRACK!
Out jumped a little yellow duck.

"Well, what is this?" said the little duck
when he saw the bunny.
"What could this little fur thing be?"

The bunny was very sleepy,
so he was still asleep
and didn't wake up.

"Inside the egg,"
said the duck,
"I thought I was all alone
in a small dark world.

"Now I find myself alone with a bunny
in a big bright world.
And the bunny won't wake up."

So the duck pushed the

bunny with his foot

And jumped
on top of him

And threw a little rock
at him

And rolled him down a hill.

And the bunny woke up.
"Where is my egg?"
said the bunny.
"And where did you
come from?"

"Never mind that," said the duck.
"Here I am."
So the bunny and the duck
were friends

And no one was ever
alone again.

ANIMAL FRIENDS

Once upon a time, in a small house deep in the woods, lived a lively family of animals.

There were Miss Kitty and Mr. Pup, Brown Bunny, Little Chick, Fluffy Squirrel, Poky Turtle, and Tweeter Bird.

Each had his little chest and his little bed and chair, and they took turns cooking on their little kitchen stove.

They got along nicely when it came to sharing toys, being quiet at nap times and keeping the house neat. But they could not agree on food.

When Miss Kitty cooked, they had milk and catnip tea and little bits of liver on their plates.

Pup didn't mind the liver, but the rest were unhappy.

And they didn't like any better the juicy bones Pup
served them in his turn.

When Bunny fixed the meals, she arranged lettuce leaves and carrot nibbles with artistic taste, but only Tweeter Bird would eat any of them. And when Tweeter served worms, and crispy, chewy seeds, only Little Chick would eat them.

Little Chick liked bugs and beetles even better. Poky Turtle would nibble at them, but what he really hungered for were tasty ants' eggs.

Fluffy Squirrel wanted nuts and nuts and nuts. Without his sharp teeth and his firm paws, the others could not get a nibble from a nut, so they all went hungry when Fluffy got the meals.

Finally they all knew something must be done. They gathered around the fire one cool and cozy evening and talked things over.

"The home for me," said Mr. Pup, wistfully, "is a place where I can have lots of bones and meat every day."

"I want milk and liver instead of bugs and seeds," said Miss Kitty, daintily smoothing her skirt. "That's the kind of home for me."

"Nuts for me," said Squirrel. "And I'll get them myself."

"Ants' eggs," yawned Turtle.

"Crispy lettuce," whispered Bunny.

"A stalk of seeds," dreamed Bird, "and some worms make a home for me."

"New homes are what we need," said Mr. Pup. And everyone agreed.

So bright and early next morning they packed their little satchels and they said their fond good-by's.

Squirrel did not pack. He waved good-by to them all. For he had decided to stay in the house in the woods.

He started right in to gather nuts.

Soon there were nuts in the kitchen stove, nuts in the cupboards, nuts piled up in all the empty beds. There was scarcely room for that happy little Squirrel.

The others hopped along till they came to a garden with rows and rows of tasty growing things. "Here's the home for me," said bright-eyed Brown Bunny, and she settled down there at the roots of a big tree.

Little Chick found a chicken yard full of lovely scratchy gravel where lived all kinds of crispy, crunchy bugs.

"Here I stay," chirped Chick, squeezing under the fence to join the other chickens there.

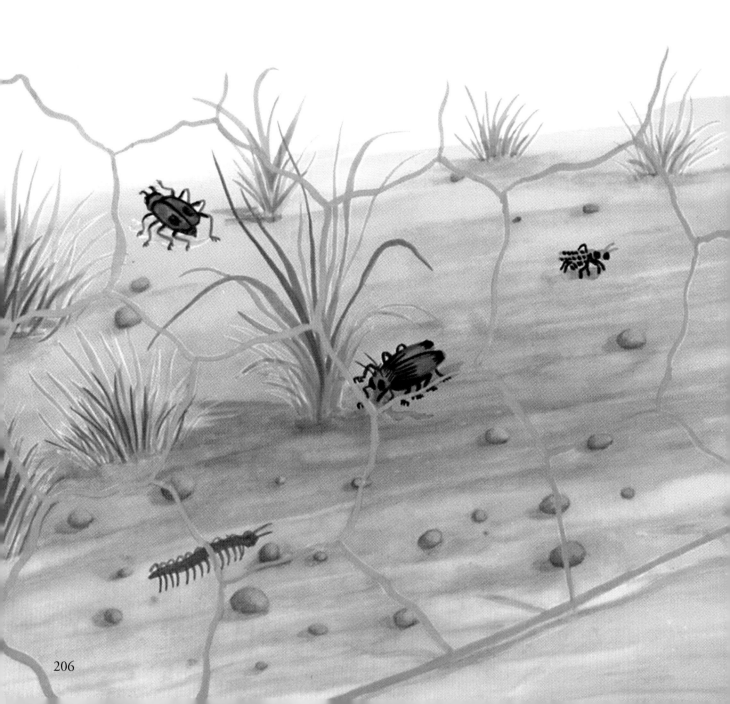

207

Poky Turtle found a pond with a lovely log for napping, half in the sun, half in the shade.

Close by the log was a busy, bustling ant hill, full of the eggs Turtle loved.

Tweeter Bird found a nest in a tree above the pond, where he could see the world, the seeds on the grasses, and the worms on the ground.

"This is the home for me," sang Bird happily.

Miss Kitty went on till she came to a house where
a little girl welcomed her.

"Here is a bowl of milk for you, Miss Kitty," said
the little girl, "and a ball of yarn to play with."

So Miss Kitty settled down in her new home with
a purr.

Mr. Pup found a boy in the house next door.
The boy had a bone and some meat for Pup, a bed
for him to sleep in, and a handsome collar to wear.
    "Bow wow," barked Pup. "This is the home
for me."

That night each one said, as he went to sleep, "At last I've found the best of all, the very best home for me."

The BIG BROWN BEAR

Once there was a big brown bear who lived with
his wife inside a cave.

"Please, dear," she said to him one day, "run down to the brook and catch some fish for dinner. But don't go near the beehive in the old dead tree. Remember what they did to you last time."

And the bear's wife lit the fire and took down her
frying pan.

Meanwhile, the big brown bear walked slowly down the path toward the brook. Of course, he had no intention of even looking at the hive.

But before he knew it, there he was heading straight for the old dead tree! He sniffed the good smell of honey and it made him walk faster, and the faster he walked, the better it smelled.

As soon as he reached the tree, he pushed his paw into the hive and grabbed a piece of honeycomb. Inside, the busy bees were making wax and honey.

But the minute they saw that big paw wrecking their
home and stealing their precious honey, they rushed out,
darting in all directions and droning like a million airplanes.

The bear yanked out his paw. Then he let out a big
roar, and he ran away so fast that he left the bees far
behind him.

Alas, he caught his foot in the root of a tree and tumbled over and over and rolled down the hill into a thorn bush.

Swarming after him in a big cloud, the bees were ready to zoom down on his head. So the poor bear had to act fast. Pulling and kicking and tugging, he tore himself loose at last, leaving a great deal of his fur in the bush.

He ran toward the brook, jumped into the water, and hid there with only his nose showing. The water was very chilly, but he didn't dare to move.

The bees circled around and around, looking for him everywhere. Suddenly they spotted him under the water, and they swooped down and landed smack on his nose.

"Ouch!" he yelled. "Ouch! Ouch!"

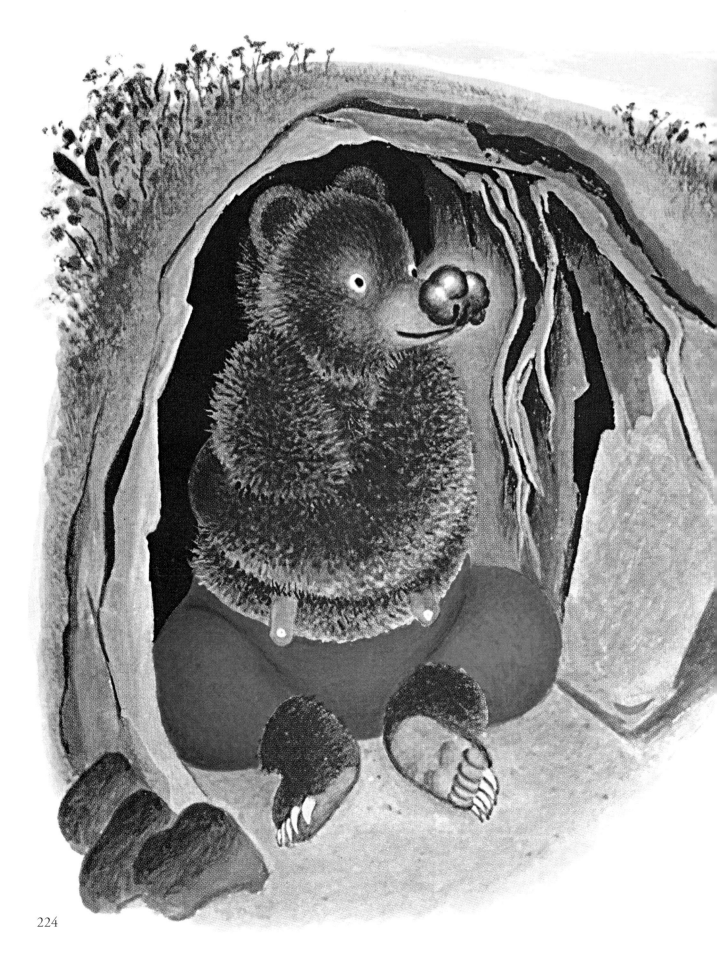

Quickly the brown bear scrambled out of the water and crawled into a deep hole under the bank. He sat in the dark, all wet and shivering, with his nose getting bigger and bigger.

After a long time, very cautiously, he took a peep outside. He didn't see any bees, he didn't hear any bees, and of course he couldn't smell any bees because his nose was too sore and swollen. So he crawled out, an inch at a time, and found himself in the sunshine again.

And he was supposed to catch some fish for dinner!

So he knelt on a rock and looked in the water and saw a big trout. She kept very still, but the bear saw her and caught her with one flip of his paw.

It made him feel much better. The trout looked even bigger out of the water, and the bear was so pleased he couldn't wait to show her to his wife.

But halfway home, as he was going past the old dead
tree, he heard the bees, who were still fighting mad.
They were buzzing around the hive.

The brown bear crouched down and crept through the
tall grass, trying to make himself invisible.

When he was far from the tree, he straightened up and raced back to his cave, looking over his shoulder from time to time.

He was so happy to be home that he gave his wife a great big bear hug and kissed her on both ears. His wife was quite surprised by such a greeting and guessed right away that he had done something wrong.

And as soon as she saw his nose, she knew what he had done.

"Oh, dear!" she cried. "Why did you go near those bees?"

The brown bear had nothing to say for himself except to promise that he would never, never go anywhere near the old dead tree again.

His wife put a wet compress on his nose. Then she cooked the trout and gave him the biggest piece.

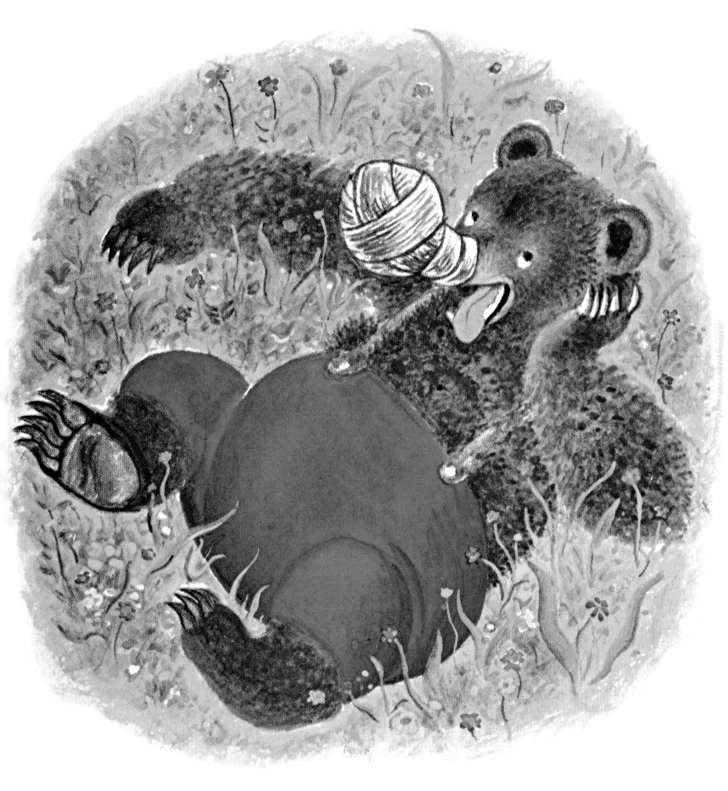

"It's the best trout I ever ate," said the big brown bear.
But way deep inside, he wished he had some of that
nice honey for dessert.

"Spring, Spring, Spring!"
sang the frog.
  "Spring!" said the groundhog.

"Spring, Spring, Spring!"
sang the robin.

It was Spring.

The leaves burst out.

The flowers burst out.

And robins burst out of their eggs.

It was Spring.

In the Spring a bunny
came down the road.
   He was going to find
a home of his own.
   A home for a bunny,
   A home of his own,
   Under a rock,
   Under a stone,
   Under a log,
   Or under the ground.
   Where would a bunny find a home?

243

"Where is your home?"
he asked the robin.

"Here, here, here,"
sang the robin.
"Here in this nest is my home."

"Here, here, here,"
sang the little robins who were
about to fall out of the nest.
"Here is our home."

"Not for me," said the bunny.
"I would fall out of a nest.
I would fall on the ground."

So he went on
looking for a home.
"Where is your home?"
he asked a frog.

"Wog, wog, wog,"
sang the frog.
"Wog, wog, wog,
Under the water,
Down in the bog."
  "Not for me,"
said the bunny.
"Under the water,
I would drown in a bog."

So he went on
looking for a home.
"Where do you live?"
he asked the groundhog.
"In a log," said the groundhog.
"Can I come in?" said the bunny.
"No, you can't come in my log,"
said the groundhog.

So the bunny went down the road.
   Down the road
and down the road he went.
   He was going to find
a home of his own.
   A home for a bunny,
   A home of his own,
   Under a rock
   Or a log
   Or a stone.
   Where would a bunny find a home?

Down the road
and down the road
and down the road
he went, until—

He met a bunny.
"Where is your home?"
he asked the bunny.

"Here," said the bunny.
"Here is my home.
Under this rock,
Under this stone,
Down under the ground,
Here is my home."

"Can I come in?"
said the bunny.
"Yes," said the bunny.
And so he did.

And that was his home.

How the Camel Got Its Hump

TALES FROM AROUND THE WORLD

Welcome! I am Shari Zodd, and I know a thousand and one tales!

Today I will tell you some camel tales, for the camel is a most amazing animal. Every part of its body is just right for life in the hot, cold, windy, and dry, dry, *dry* desert.

But no part of the camel's body is more amazing than its hump! How did the camel get its hump? Listen, and I will tell you.

The great storyteller Aesop says the camel was created by the mighty Greek god Zeus.

One day, Horse asked Zeus for a longer neck, a broader chest, and a built-in saddle.

The next thing Horse knew, why, he'd become
a camel! But if you think that would satisfy the
camel, you do not know camels.

The Chinese tell a tale of Camel asking the Creator for broad feet for walking on shifting sands, long eyelashes for keeping out wind, and a hump or two for carrying food and water.

The Creator granted all of this. But was the camel happy? No! Because all the other animals laughed at its funny-looking humps.

The camel asked to have its homely humps removed, but this could not be done. "How can I go on with all the other animals looking down on me?" wailed the camel.

"You shall look down on them!" thundered the Creator.

From that day on, camels had such a haughty look that no animal ever dared laugh at them again. And camels still have their hairy humps, which come in handy in the desert, as you will learn in my next tale.

Long ago, there lived a bandit and his hardworking camel. Day and night they rode over the endless, shifting sands.

They rode in the heat of day . . .

. . . They traveled through the cold of night. They rode into whirling sandstorms.

Camel's feet became flat from walking. Its eyelashes grew long from squinting. Its chest and knees grew furry from resting on the cold ground.

Camel became strong from carrying heavy
sacks of food, water, and coins.

But never once did the bandit share his food
or water with poor Camel. So Camel learned to
do without, except for what it could find in the
dry, dry, *dry* desert.

One day, Camel's broad foot bumped a magic lamp that contained a genie! As everyone knows, if you ever find a genie, it will give you three wishes. So the bandit snatched the lamp and asked the genie for 50 bags of wealth and 50 years of health.

Before he could make his third wish, Camel grunted, "I walked us here. I found the lamp. I want a wish!"

"Very well," said the genie. "What do you command?"

Camel said, "I wish the water I carried was for myself."

Instantly, Camel had its hump!

And the bandit had his 50 bags of wealth. But he didn't pay taxes on it. So the bandit was sent to jail, where he was always thirsty, for 50 years.

But a camel is never thirsty—unless it forgets to fill its hump.

But what about the most famous camel-got-its-hump story, the one by Rudyard Kipling? That story takes place when the world was so new that there were only a few animals, including the lazy camel. During the first three days of the world, the other animals worked very hard.

Then Horse asked Camel to trot with him. But Camel said, *"Humph!"*

Dog asked Camel to help him fetch and carry. But Camel said, *"Humph!"*

Ox asked Camel to help him plow. But Camel said, *"Humph!"*

The animals begged the Djinn, or Genie, of All Deserts to do something about the lazy camel.

"He won't trot," said Horse.

"He won't fetch," said Dog.

"He won't plow," said Ox. "He just says, *'Humph!'"*

"I'll *humph* him, if you'll kindly wait a minute," said the genie. *"Alakazam!"*

To the camel the genie said, "Do you see that? That's your very own 'humph' that you brought on your very own self by not working."

"How can I work with a hump on my back?" the camel humphed.

The genie explained, "You can work three times harder because you can live off your hump." And the camel still works three times harder, because it has never caught up with the three days that it missed at the beginning of the world.

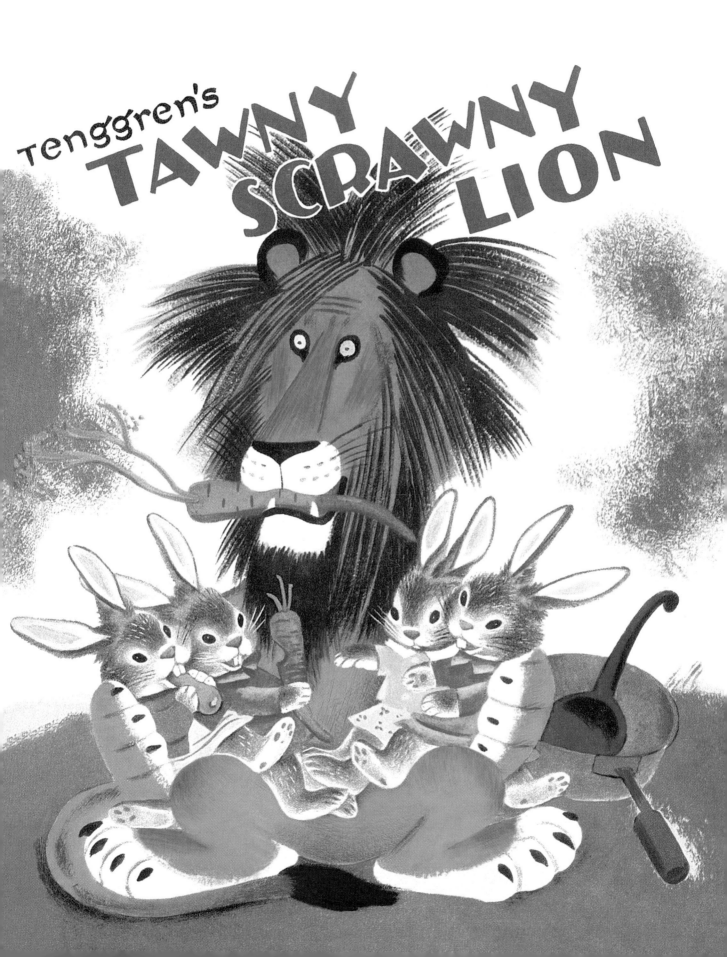

Tenggren's TAWNY SCRAWNY LION

Once there was a tawny, scrawny, hungry lion who never could get enough to eat.

He chased monkeys on Monday—

kangaroos on Tuesday—

zebras on Wednesday—

bears on Thursday—

camels on Friday—

and on Saturday, elephants!

And since he caught everything he ran after, that lion should have been as fat as butter. But he wasn't at all. The more he ate, the scrawnier and hungrier he grew.

The other animals didn't feel one bit safe. They stood at a distance and tried to talk things over with the tawny, scrawny lion.

"It's all your fault for running away," he grumbled. "If I didn't have to run, run, run for every single bite I get, I'd be fat as butter and

sleek as satin. Then I wouldn't have to eat so much, and you'd last longer!"

Just then, a fat little rabbit came hopping through the forest, picking berries. All the big animals looked at him and grinned slyly.

"Rabbit," they said. "Oh, you lucky rabbit! We appoint you to talk things over with the lion."

That made the little rabbit feel very proud.

"What shall I talk about?" he asked eagerly.

"Any old thing," said the big animals. "The important thing is to go right up close."

So the fat little rabbit hopped right up to the big hungry lion and counted his ribs.

"You look much too scrawny to talk things over," he said. "So how about supper at my house first?"

"What's for supper?" asked the lion.

The little rabbit said, "Carrot stew." That sounded awful to the lion. But the little rabbit said, "Yes sir, my five fat sisters and my four fat

brothers are making a delicious big carrot stew right now!"

"What are we waiting for?" cried the lion. And he went hopping away with the little rabbit, thinking of ten fat rabbits, and looking just as jolly as you please.

"Well," grinned all the big animals. "That should take care of Tawny-Scrawny for today."

Before very long, the lion began to wonder if they would ever get to the rabbit's house.

First, the fat little rabbit kept stopping to pick berries and mushrooms and all sorts of good-smelling herbs. And when his basket was full, what did he do but flop down on the river bank!

"Wait a bit," he said.

"I want to catch a few fish for the stew."

That was almost too much for the hungry lion.

For a moment, he thought he would have to eat that one little rabbit then and there. But he kept saying "five fat sisters and four fat brothers" over and over to himself. And at last the two were on their way again.

"Here we are!" said the rabbit, hopping around a turn with the lion close behind him. Sure enough, there was the rabbit's house, with a big pot of carrot stew bubbling over an open fire.

And sure enough, there were nine more fat, merry little rabbits hopping around it!

When they saw the fish, they popped them into the stew, along with the mushrooms and herbs. The stew began to smell very good indeed.

And when they saw the tawny, scrawny lion, they gave him a big bowl of hot stew. And then they hopped about so busily, that really, it would have been quite a job for that tired, hungry lion to catch even one of them!

So he gobbled his stew, but the rabbits filled his bowl again. When he had eaten all he could hold, they heaped his bowl with berries.

And when the berries were gone—the tawny, scrawny lion wasn't scrawny any more! He felt so good and fat and comfortable that he couldn't even move.

"Here's a fine thing!" he said to himself. "All these fat little rabbits, and I haven't room inside for even one!"

He looked at all those fine, fat little rabbits and wished he'd get hungry again.

"Mind if I stay a while?" he asked.

"We wouldn't even hear of your going!" said the rabbits. Then they plumped themselves down in the lion's lap and began to sing songs.

And somehow, even when it was time to say goodnight, that lion wasn't one bit hungry!

Home he went, through the soft moonlight, singing softly to himself. He curled up in his bed, patted his sleek, fat tummy, and smiled.

When he woke up in the morning, it was Monday.

"Time to chase monkeys!" said the lion.

But he wasn't one bit hungry for monkeys! What he wanted was some more of that tasty carrot stew. So off he went to visit the rabbits.

On Tuesday he didn't want kangaroos, and on Wednesday he didn't want zebras. He wasn't hungry for bears on Thursday, or camels on Friday, or elephants on Saturday.

All the big animals were so surprised and happy! They dressed in their best and went to see the fat little rabbit.

"Rabbit," they said. "Oh, you wonderful rabbit! What in the world did you talk to the tawny, scrawny, hungry, terrible lion about?"

The fat little rabbit jumped up in the air and said, "Oh, my goodness! We had such a good time with that nice, jolly lion that I guess we forgot to talk about anything at all!"

And before the big animals could say one word,
the tawny lion came skipping up the path. He had

a basket of berries for the fat rabbit sisters, and a string of fish for the fat rabbit brothers, and a big bunch of daisies for the fat rabbit himself.

"I came for supper," he said, shaking paws all around.

Then he sat down in the soft grass, looking fat as butter, sleek as satin, and jolly as all get out, all ready for another good big supper of carrot stew.

308